D1540653

Ears Like Gramps

Written by Margie Harding
Illustrated by Jennifer Phipps

THIS BOOK IS DEDICATED TO "HUNTER"

"Paxton, can you turn the TV up?" asked Owen Owl, as the friends enjoyed their favorite show, *Animal Friends*, together. "I can hardly hear it."

"I think it's loud enough," said Liam Mountain Lion. "You going deaf?" Liam teased.

"Of course I'm not going deaf," snapped Owen. "The TV is just not loud enough!"

"We can turn it up some," said Paxton Prairie Dog. "I don't mind."

"I still can't hear it. I'm going home," said Owen.

"I can walk with you," said Eli Elk. "I'm supposed to be home in fifteen minutes anyway."

"I'm leaving, too," said Paxton. "We'll see you tomorrow," he said, as the friends left for home.

The three friends parted ways at the crossroad. Owen stopped when he saw Roscoe Raccoon coming out of the brush. "I called you. Didn't you hear me?" asked Roscoe.

"Nope, I didn't. I must have been daydreaming," Owen said cheerfully, while trying to hide how frightened he was.

"It's okay," said Roscoe. "I'm headed home anyway. It's time for dinner."

"Me too. I'll talk with you later."

Owen watched while Roscoe went into the thicket and then shook his head really hard. "What is wrong with me? Why didn't I hear him call me? Is Liam right? Am I going deaf?"

"It's about time you came home," said Owen's mom. "I was beginning to get worried."

"Why?"

"You were supposed to be home an hour ago. I told you before you left to only be gone about an hour because your dad and I have plans for tonight."

"You did? I didn't hear you say that."

"What is wrong with you? You haven't been paying attention for days now!"

"I don't know. I feel kind of funny sometimes," said Owen.

"What do you mean, funny?"

Owen stopped and stared out over the field. "I don't know. Just funny!"

"Well, there's no time to worry about it now. Here's your dinner. Your dad and I will return in a couple hours. Aunt Olivia, next door, will keep an eye out for you. If you need anything, call her."

"I'll be fine," said Owen.

"I'm sure you will," said his mother, walking out the door.

Owen ate his dinner and flew to the branch above their home. He drank in the beauty of this place he called home, when in an instant he found himself on the ground unable to move. "Aunt Olivia!" called Owen. "Aunt Olivia! I need your help."

"You've broken your wing," said Dr. Avery Antelope, a little while later. "What were you doing?"

"Nothing! Honest! I just flew up onto the branch above our home. I've done that all my life. And then I had that funny feeling again. And then next thing I knew I was on the ground."

"What funny feeling?"

"I don't know. Just funny. Not ha-ha funny, but weird funny."

"He mentioned that "funny feeling" earlier today," said Momma Oralee Owl, who arrived after Olivia phoned her about the accident.

"Let me check a few things," said Dr. Avery.

Dr. Avery looked into Owen's eyes and then he checked Owen's ears.

"Hmmmmm," said Dr. Avery. "Have you been having any hearing issues?"

"I don't know," he answered, thinking hard. "I didn't hear Roscoe call me earlier today. And I did want the TV louder when we were watching it. So maybe," he said, shrugging his shoulders.

"Ohhh," he said feeling the pain from the broken wing.

"It looks like you have something called Otitis Media, and maybe even some bigger issues."

"What's O-ti-tis Me-di-a?" asked Owen.

"Otitis Media is an infection in the ear where fluid builds up, causing hearing loss and even sometimes balance issues, which is what might have happened to you on your branch today. You lost your balance causing you to fall."

"He's had this problem before, even often when he was younger, but it's been a while," said Momma.

"Will it go away, Dr. Avery?" asked Owen. "Will I be able to hear right again?"

"I believe you will, but we might have to look at some other options to help you be able to hear."

"You mean there are long term effects from this problem, Dr. Avery?" asked Momma.

"I'm afraid so," said Dr. Avery, gravely. "This repeated problem with fluid build up and infection can cause damage to the eardrum. The bones in the ear and nerves can also be affected, causing permanent hearing loss. I need to run more tests, but I'm reasonably certain, Owen is going to need hearing aids."

"What's a hearing aid?" asked Owen.

"It's a device worn on or near the ear that allows people to hear. It has a special microphone that picks up sounds that travel through a small plastic tube, that also helps hold the hearing aid in place."

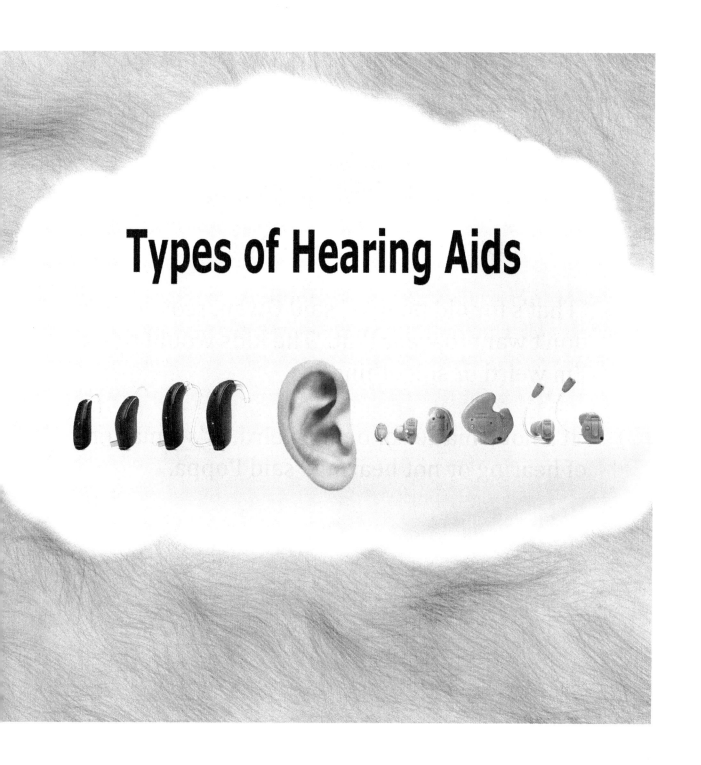

Types of Hearing Aids

"You mean like Gramps wears?"

"Yes," answered Poppa Oren Owl.

"That's for old people," said Owen, scowling. "I don't want to wear that. The kids would think I'm weird or something."

"It's not a matter of being weird. It's a matter of hearing or not hearing," said Poppa.

"There is a new kind of hearing aid," explained Dr. Avery, "that should correct the problem, yet be hardly visible."

"Can't I just have medicine again and not have the hearing aid?"

"I think this time, there is enough hearing loss that you will need to use a hearing aid if you want to hear well. Let me do some tests and we'll see."

Several weeks later, after a variety of hearing screenings, Owen went to see Dr. Avery. "Here are your hearing aids," said Dr. Avery, as Owen sat on the table.

"Will they really make me hear better?" Owen asked.

"Yes, they will. Your hearing loss is not as severe as some children, but it is progressive. It seems you have some bone structure issues that is also part of the original ear infection problem, but we should be able to manage your hearing loss now."

Dr. Avery placed the tiny hearing aids in Owen's ears. "That feels funny," said Owen.

"You will get used to it in no time, and you won't be falling off branches anymore," said Dr. Avery, patting Owen's wing sling.

"How is your wing feeling?"

Owen's eyes brightened. "I heard you really clear!" he said, ignoring Dr. Avery's question. "How did you do that?"

"It's your hearing aids. They will need some adjusting, but we'll get it just right and you'll hear as good as anyone."

"I can't wait to tell Paxton and the others!" said Owen, excitedly. "I'll be able to hear the TV now and Ms. Mira Mink at school and hear everybody when they talk to me. This is awesome," he added! "Just awesome!"

Resource Page

For additional information, visit the sites below.

(The author is in no way affiliated with these websites)

www.deafchildren.org
www.babyhearing.org
www.agbell.org
www.cdc.gov
www.hearingloss.org

CPSIA information can be obtained
at www.ICGtesting.com
Printed in the USA
BVOW07s0038170416
444500BV00001B/1/P